*North American Indian song*
Here I am
behold me
I am the sun
behold me.

Here I am
behold me
it said as it rose
I am the moon
behold me.

*Author's note:*
This North American Indian myth comes from the Kutenai, a people who once
lived on the plains of Montana. They tell many stories about Coyote the Trickster.
This is one of them.

Copyright © Joanna Troughton 1985

*First published in 1985 and reprinted in 1989 by*
Blackie and Son Ltd.,
7 Leicester Place, London WC2H 7BP

*First American edition published in 1985 by*
Peter Bedrick Books, 2112 Broadway, New York, NY 10023

British Library Cataloguing in Publication Data
Troughton, Joanna
Who will be the sun?
1. Indians of North America——Legends
I. Title    398.2'1'097  PZ8.1
ISBN 0-216-91720-4

Library of Congress Cataloging in Publication Data
Troughton, Joanna
Who will be the sun?
Summary: Raven, Chicken Hawk, and Coyote, and other
animals vie for the honor of being the sun and bringing
light to their dark world.
1. Kutenai Indians——Legends  2. Indians of North
America——Montana——Legends.  3. Coyote (Legendary
character)——Juvenile literature.  (1. Kutenai Indians——
Legends.  2. Indians of North America——Montana——
Legends.  3. Animals——Fiction)  I. Title
E99.K85T76  1986    398'.369974442 (E)  (398.2) 85-15074
ISBN 0-87226-038-0

*Printed in Italy*

# Who will be the Sun?

*Retold and illustrated by*

## Joanna Troughton

Blackie
London

Bedrick/Blackie
New York

Once it was always dark.
"Who will be the sun?"
asked the Chief of
the Indians.

Raven said, "Let it be me."
In the morning the animals watched
for him to come up.

Raven came up but he was not bright enough.
The day looked black.
"You cannot be the sun," said the Chief
of the Indians.

Chicken Hawk said, "I will be the sun."
Chicken Hawk went up. When he went up
high the sky became yellow.

"You cannot be the sun," said the Chief of the Indians. "You make the weather look bad."

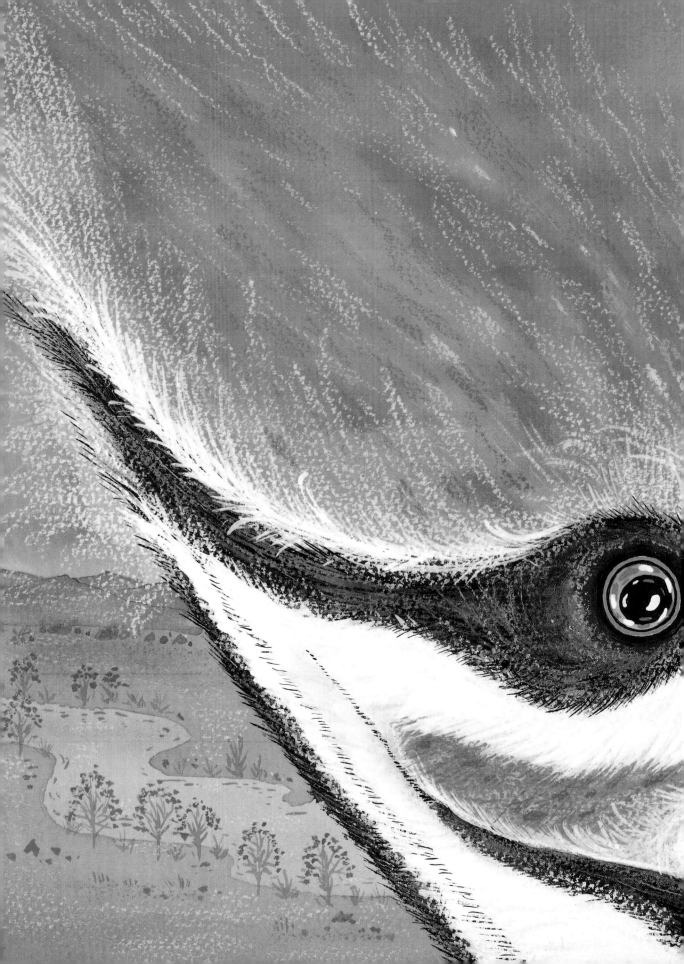

Woodpecker went up next. "I will be the sun," he said. But when he went up the world was reddish.
"You cannot be the sun," said the Chief of the Indians. "The day looks too red."

Coyote said, "I will be the sun."
Coyote was a hot-head. He always
talked too much.

Next morning Coyote went up.
When he started the day began
to be hot.

At noon it was very hot. Shade was made,
but the shade was always hot. The
children were put into the river,
but even the water was hot. Some of the
animals hid under stones.

Ermine had the tip of his tail burnt.
Mountain goat went into a cave and
stayed white. The animals who didn't hide
scorched their backs, so their
stomachs are always paler now.

Coyote was a gossip.
He saw everything the animals did and told tales.

At night Coyote came back. "You cannot be the sun," said the Chief of the Indians. "You are too hot and you talk too much. You are a bad sun."

There were two Lynx brothers. The elder Lynx was bigger. He said, "I will be the sun." He went up. In the morning the air was coolish. He went up higher and the day always felt comfortable.

At noon it became warm, but the shade was cool and the water was not hot.

In the evening Lynx came down. "You can be the sun," said the Chief of the Indians.

Coyote was jealous. He took his bow and
arrow to the place where the sun comes up.
He aimed at the sun.

But Lynx saw Coyote and burned his arrow.
It burned quickly and Coyote threw it away.
Then everything was on fire.

The fire followed Coyote, and he found a trail and lay down on it. There was no grass on the trail, so the fire went each side and Coyote was saved.

From that time the people have always found a trail to lie down on when there is a fire.

So it was decided that Lynx should be
the sun, and his younger brother should
be the moon. But it is Coyote who is
always the trickster.